# THE MAGICAL KINGDOM OF ING
## AN ENCHANTING TALE OF FAIRIES AND DRAGONS

# SUSAN BROUGHER

"And as the seasons come and go,
here's something you might like to know.
There are fairies everywhere:
under bushes, in the air,
playing games just like you play,
singing through their busy day.
So listen, touch, and look around —
in the air and on the ground.
And if you watch all nature's things,
you might just see a fairy's wing."
~Author Unknown


The Kingdom of Ing is an enchanted place where dragons are playful and kind. It is surrounded by fairies who protect the kingdom with their magical powers.

Long, long ago and far, far away

in the Magical Kingdom of Ing

under the moon in the darkness of night

lay the sweet, loving queen

dreaming, sighing,

and weeping.

At the top of the tower

her tears gently flowing,

rolled out of the castle and into the forest

covering the ground

in a mist all around.

Pictures of mothers mothering

hung on the walls

of long, winding halls

reminding the queen

of baby Ing things,

kissing and hugging,

and late good-night snuggling.

Early each morning

she went on her way

dressed in a gown,

royal purple and blue,

her silken cape trailing,

while serving and tending

to dragon lng crowds

who were praising and bending.

She rode in her carriage

smiling and waving

as mighty white horses

pulled, prancing and neighing.

There were affairs in the castle

with dancing and singing,

and tiny dragon babies

to bless when receiving.

Years went by racing

as mighty King Alexander

and his loving Queen Arabella

knelt, hoping and praying

that they would be bringing

a sweet baby dragon

into the kingdom

one day to be leading.

Bibs for burping

and blankets for warming

in the nursery sat waiting

with a cradle for rocking,

and books about trying,

helping, and flying.

The dragons believing

that a prince or a princess

they'd soon be needing

sent whispers wide-spreading

into the forest and over the mountains

sprinkling on fairies

skipping and playing.

Proudly wearing his crown

and a velvety cape,

King Alexander,

secretly worrying,

came stepping, eyes flashing,

and firmly declaring,

"Send in the fairies before it's too late!"

Hearing him bellow

and loudly commanding,

the fairies in clusters

came zigging and zagging,

wings beating and bobbing,

passing turtles slow-moving,

frogs croak-croaking, and owls

hoot-hooting.

Come closer and listen.

Ears will be tickling

and fairy bells ringing.

Alannah, the queen of fairies,

is calling

her very best team.

Tea Cup,

Looking Glass,

and Busy Bee,

her handpicked

chosen three,

gathered, planning, exploring,

then eagerly going.

Tea Cup sat gazing,

thinking and wondering,

sipping on tea

that was steaming

and foaming,

when in a moment

her plans spread unfolding.

Holding on to each other's hands

off they all flew

dipping and diving,

landing into

the caves deep below

where the lost orphans go.

Safely they slept in the arms

of mothering mothers

each baby dreaming

of living above

with their own mother lng

to love and be loved.

The fairies sat pondering

wishing to take everyone.

Looking Glass, slipping and sliding

over big puddles toe-tipping,

her tiny shoes dripping,

discovered a sweet orphan boy,

dreaming, sighing, and weeping,

his tears gently flowing

out of the cave and into the forest

covering the ground in a mist all around.

Busy Bee, whipping and whirling

her tiny wings, swirling

faster and faster,

wildly unfurling,

went swooping and scooping

the sad baby boy.

With a tear in each eye

up, up they all flew

out of the cave

and safely into

the tallest of trees they could find.

Stretching baby Ing's blanket

snug round his belly

and pulling it tight

in their small fairy hands,

they slipped through the clouds

and soared out of sight

under the moon in the darkness of night

to the top of the tower and into the room

of their sweet, loving queen.

There in the shadows three fairies of light

opened baby Ing's blanket

blowing see-you-soon kisses

on his plump bumpy head,

and placing him softly

into the bed

of their sweet, loving queen.

They floated midair, watching her dream.

No cries could be heard

as she slumbered.

No tears

left her saucer-brown eyes.

Her murmuring sighs

went drifting

down into the streets

and floating up into the skies.


THE END

This happy story has come to an end, but as is true with so many things in the Magical Kingdom of Ing, when one story stops, another takes wing. There is a prince in the castle needing a name for his father the king to proclaim. There will be lots of books about helping and trying, and look out below, there will be lessons in flying.

The three fairies hold special gifts. Can you guess what they might be? Keep reading to find out, or make up your own.

Tea Cup, when sipping on tea, imagines what needs to be done and quickly makes a plan.

Looking Glass gazes into the future and finds what is lost that others can't see.

Busy Bee, while spinning her wings faster and faster, gets stronger and stronger.

Can you count the "ing's" on each page? Do you know what "ing" means? It is complicated, but we can make it simple. In the Kingdom of Ing, it means "belonging together."

CPSIA information can be obtained
at www.ICGtesting.com
Printed in the USA
BVHW020846150620
581520BV00002B/60